D0618248

For the Wild sisters

One field poppy plant can produce as many as 50,000 seeds. Which goes to show that even something very small can make a BIG difference.
—F.W.

Copyright © 2018 by Fiona Woodcock · All rights reserved. Published in the United States by Random House Children's Books, a division of Penguin Random House LLC, New York. Published simultaneously in hardcover in Great Britain by Simon & Schuster UK, London. · Random House and the colophon are registered trademarks of Penguin Random House LLC. · Visit us on the Web! randomhousekids.com · Educators and librarians, for a variety of teaching tools, visit us at RHTeachersLibrarians.com · Library of Congress Cataloging-in-Publication Data is available upon request. · ISBN 978-1-5247-6967-3
MANUFACTURED IN CHINA
10 9 8 7 6 5 4 3 2 1
First American Edition

Random House Children's Books supports the First Amendment and celebrates the right to read.

Poppy, Buttercup, Bluebell & Dandy

by Fiona Woodcock

Random House 🏠 New York

On top of a hill, not far from here,
live *Poppy* and her friends.

There's *Dandy* and *Bluebell*

and bright little *Buttercup*.

Together they run wild,
spreading sunshine wherever they go!

One morning, Poppy woke up with a strange tingling feeling. It fluttered in her tummy and shivered the tips of her petals.

"Hop on your wheels, Blooms!" she said.
"We've got to head to the city!"

It wasn't long before they saw the sign.
Buttercup's glow lit up the words.

Today's the day—
LAST PARK IN THE CITY
TO BE CLOSED.

"*We have to save the park!*" cried Poppy.
"But where is it?" said Dandy. "The city is so big.
How will we find our way?"

"*Follow me!*" said Poppy.
"If we go higher up,
we can look for the park!"

"Keep climbing, Buttercup,"
said Dandy breathlessly.

"*We're nearly there,*"
called Bluebell.

"*We made it!*" said Poppy.
"Can anyone see the park?"
But then . . .

"STOP!" cried Poppy.
"Now what are we going to do?" said Dandy,
who wished they could just go home.

"Well," said Poppy, "it looks like there's only one way to go . . ."

"*. . . and it's down!*"

Bluebell edged her skateboard forward.
"Oooh, this will be fun!" She grinned and . . .

Wheeeeeeeeeeee!

"It's soft, but very smelly!" said Bluebell,
giggling as she landed in the dump.

Picking themselves up, the four
friends sped through alleyways
and down dim side streets,
the wheels on their
skateboards whirring.

"Come on!" whooped Poppy. "The park
has to be just around the corner!"

Whoa!
"A car!" shouted Poppy. "Quick! This way!"

They scrambled to safety,
up and up and up.

"Where does this end?"
asked Dandy as Buttercup
lit the way.

At last they reached the top.
They could see the park—but now it was far, far below.
"I'm tired," said Dandy.
"There must be a way down there," said Poppy. "I'm sure of it."
"How?" said Buttercup.

"Quick, grab hold!"
called Bluebell.

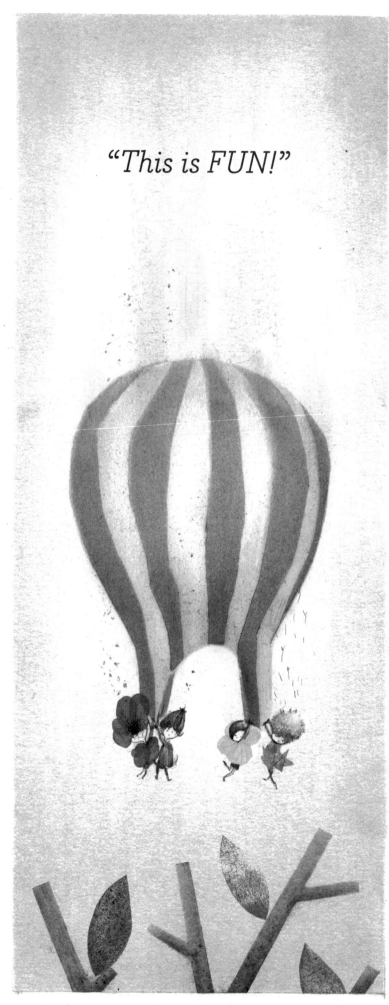

"This is FUN!"

They landed in just the right place to run wild and
spread their sunshine. "Let's get to work!" said Poppy.
So they did just that . . .

. . . and a whole lot more!

When the Blooms arrived back home after their adventure, they turned and saw just how far their magic had spread. Poppy's petals tingled once more.

"Hey, Blooms, we did that," she said, and smiled.

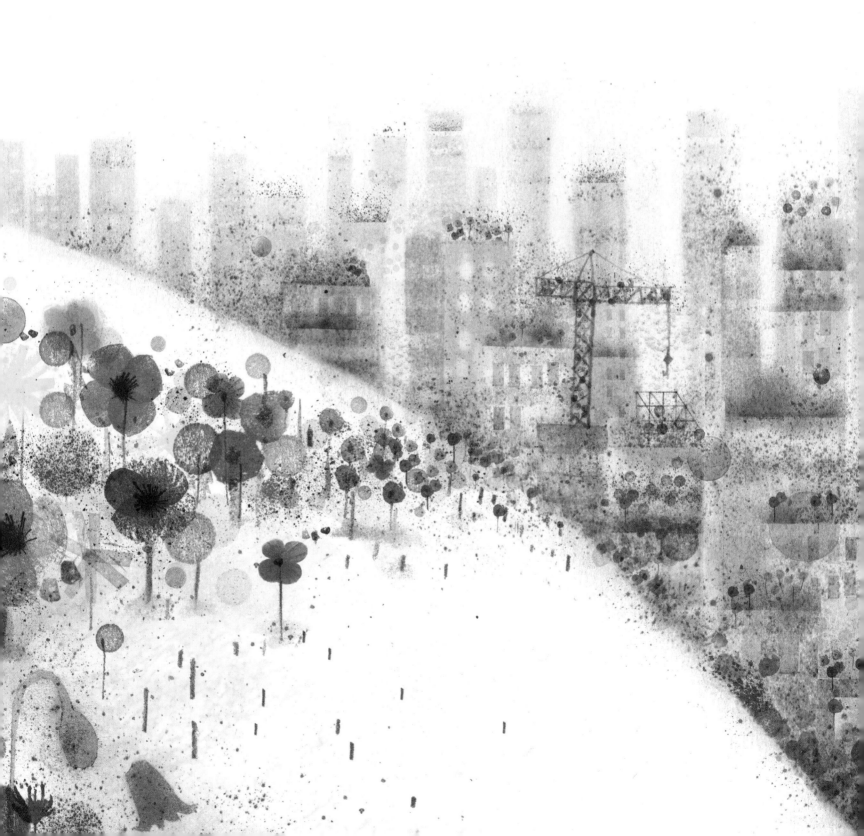

"*We did it together,*" said Dandy and Bluebell
and bright little Buttercup.